Blue's Beach Day

by Jeff Borkin
illustrated by Karen Craig

Ready-to-Read

Simon Spotlight/Nick Jr.

New York   London   Toronto   Sydney

Based on the TV series *Blue's Clues*® created by Traci Paige Johnson,
Todd Kessler, and Angela C. Santomero as seen on Nick Jr.®
On *Blue's Clues*, Joe is played by Donovan Patton. Photos by Joan Marcus.

SIMON SPOTLIGHT
An imprint of Simon & Schuster Children's Publishing Division
1230 Avenue of the Americas, New York, New York 10020
Copyright © 2004 Viacom International Inc. All rights reserved.
NICKELODEON, NICK JR., *Blue's Clues*, and all related titles, logos, and characters are
trademarks of Viacom International Inc.
All rights reserved, including the right of reproduction in whole or in part in any form.
READY-TO-READ, SIMON SPOTLIGHT, and colophon are registered trademarks of
Simon & Schuster.
Manufactured in the United States of America
First Edition
2 4 6 8 10 9 7 5 3 1

Library of Congress Cataloging-in-Publication Data

Borkin, Jeff.
Blue's beach day / by Jeff Borkin ; [illustrated by] Karen Craig.—1st ed.
p. cm. —(Blue's clues. Ready-to-read ; #9)
"Based on the TV series Blue's Clues® as seen on Nick Jr.®."
Summary: Blue and her friends build a sand castle at the beach.
ISBN 0-689-86499-X (pbk.)
[1. Sand castles—Fiction. 2. Beaches—Fiction. 3. Dogs—Fiction.]
I.Craig, Karen, ill. II. Blue's clues (Television program) III. Title. IV.
Series.
PZ7.B648457 Bl 2004
[E]—dc21
2003008103

We are at the beach today!

Ooh, the sand
is hot!

But the water
is cool.

Here is a good spot.

We will make a sand castle!

Shovel digs a hole.

Pail holds the sand.

The sand castle gets bigger . . .

and bigger!

We find seashells for the sand castle.

Ta da!
The sand castle
is done!

Now we wait.

The water comes
closer . . .

and closer.

Sploosh!

Hooray!